Batty
the
Hero

More fantastic stories from Susan Gates:

Batty the Hero

Susan Gates

Illustrated by Rhian Nest James

SCHOLASTIC PRESS

For Christopher

Christopher

Scholastic Children's Books,
Commonwealth House, 1-19 New Oxford Street,
London WC1A 1NU, UK
a division of Scholastic Ltd
London ~ New York ~ Toronto ~ Sydney ~ Auckland
Mexico City ~ New Delhi ~ Hong Kong

Published in the UK by Scholastic Ltd, 1999

Text copyright © Susan Gates, 1999
Illustrations copyright © Rhian Nest James, 1999

ISBN 0 439 01001 2

Typeset by Rowland Phototypesetting Ltd, Bury St Edmunds, Suffolk
Printed by Cox & Wyman Ltd, Reading, Berks

2 4 6 8 10 9 7 5 3 1

S/A 60664

Chapter 1

Rinny the Goat

"Where is that boy?" yelled Mayamiko's mum. She was really mad. She was waving a piece of paper about.

"See what I found this morning, nailed to our mango tree!"

She waved the piece of paper under Anna's nose.

Anna read it out loud: "If you do not

do something about your goat, something bad will happen to it. Signed, Mrs S. Tambala."

"*Cha!*" said Mayamiko's mum. "That boy will be the death of me! See what he has done! He's let the goat escape into Mrs Tambala's garden. And now she's hopping mad!"

6

Rinny, the white goat, was Mayamiko's responsibility. She was very precious. She was expecting babies any day now. And Mayamiko was supposed to be looking after her. But he had gone to the swimming hole with his cousin Bernard. While he was away Rinny bit through her rope. She jumped out of the pen. Then she went into Mrs Tambala's garden and nibbled her maize and cassava plants.

Mrs Tambala was furious. She was on the warpath.

Mayamiko's mum was on the warpath too. She was spitting fire! "Where is that bad boy!"

"I think he's in the chim," said Anna.

"What again?" said Mayamiko's mum. "Is he sick or something? Has he been eating too many green mangoes? And, anyway, why does he keep going to that old chim? When we have a fine new chim inside our house?"

The old chim was behind the house. It was inside a little mud hut with a thatched roof. No one used it any more. Except Mayamiko. It was Mayamiko's favourite place.

"He won't be able to go there soon," said Mayamiko's mum. "Your dad is going to pull that chim down tomorrow. Anyway, go and fetch that boy for me.

I want to give him a piece of my mind!"

"Do I have to?" said Anna. "I hate going to that old chim. Do I really have to?"

"I have just said so!" said Mayamiko's mum sternly, waggling her finger. "Now move your bones!"

Chapter 2

Batty the Fruit Bat

Going to the old chim was a risky business.

It had no door, only a curtain. The curtain was closed. That meant somebody was inside. It could only be Mayamiko.

"*Hodie!*" called Anna, expecting her brother to call "*Hodie!*" back. But no answer came from inside the chim.

Oh, dear! thought Anna. I'm going to have to open that curtain!

This was the risky part.

But Anna knew what to do. She took a deep breath. Whisked the curtain open. Then quickly ducked down –

Something came clattering out of the chim. It looked like a flying black umbrella. It cackled like a witch. It swooped so low it almost parted her hair!

"*Aiee!*" yelled Anna, slapping her hands over her head. She could hear creaky wings. Smell a musty smell.

"That crazy bat!" yelled Anna.

The bat flew cackling into the mango tree. And hung there upside down.

Anna took her hands off her head. "I hate this horrible chim!" she yelled. "I'm glad Dad's pulling it down!"

She peered into the chim. It was
cobwebby and dark inside. But there
was no Mayamiko.

Where is that boy? she thought, as she trudged back to the house again. The whole world wants his skin!

Mayamiko knew people were after his skin. That's why he was hiding in the long elephant grass. He parted it with his hands. He watched Anna go back into the house. He watched the bat fly out of the mango tree. The bat flapped back into the chim on great, black leathery wings. He was a giant fruit bat. He roosted in the chim. His body was as long as Mayamiko's arm.

Mayamiko followed him. He pulled the curtain shut behind him and sat on the chim seat. He was safe now for a bit. Safe in his own little den. Until Mum and Mrs Tambala tracked him down.

But Mayamiko didn't give them a second thought. Something else was worrying him much much more.

"Did you hear it, Batty?" he said, looking up into the dark thatched roof. "Did you hear what Anna said? Dad's going to pull your home down!"

Batty was hanging upside down by his feet. He'd got claws on his toes. He'd even got claws on his wings. He swung slowly to and fro with his wings wrapped snugly around his body, like a black cloak.

He had a foxy face. And a snouty nose like a piglet. His fur was lovely, the colour of honey. And his shiny eyes were like two brown marbles.

He twirled on his perch. His rubbery lips were stretched in a permanent friendly grin. He did smell a bit. But Mayamiko had got used to that. Actually, he quite liked it.

"*Chink, chink,*" went Batty. "*Chink, chink!*"

That was the other noise he made, apart from cackling. It was a weird high, tinkling sound. Like tapping a glass with a spoon.

"Where will you go?" said Mayamiko. "Who will I talk to?"

Mayamiko often talked to Batty. He told him all his problems. He didn't think it at all strange, telling his troubles to the fruit bat who lived in the chim. In fact, he felt really sorry for children who didn't have their own fruit bat to talk to.

"It's Rinny," he explained to Batty. "She's got me into trouble again. With Mrs Tambala this time! And it's not my fault. Rinny's a bad goat. It doesn't matter how much I watch her. She always escapes!"

"*Chink! Chink!*" tinkled Batty, as if he was sympathizing.

It was the only conversation he ever made. But that suited Mayamiko just fine. He didn't want someone to talk back to him, to nag at him or tell him off. He just wanted someone to listen. And say *chink, chink* now and again to show they were still paying attention.

"I've got to stop Dad pulling this chim down!" Mayamiko told Batty. "We like this chim, don't we?"

"Chink!"

It was their personal, private chim. If Dad pulled it down Batty would fly away for ever. Just thinking about that almost broke Mayamiko's heart.

Mayamiko reached into the pocket of his shorts and took out a squelchy-ripe mango.

"Want a mango?" he asked Batty.

He held up the mango so Batty could reach it. Batty gripped it with the hooks on his wings and slurped away at it. His face got all sticky with juice. He spat out the mango skin then dropped the seed on the floor. He was a really messy eater.

"What are we going to do, Batty?"
Mayamiko asked him, sadly.

"*Hodie!*" The curtain to the chim
twitched. "I've found you at last!" cried
a voice from outside.

Oh, no! thought Mayamiko. Mum!

The curtain swished wide open. Mum
ducked. Batty dived out, almost parting
her hair.

"That crazy bat!" yelled Mum, smoothing her hair down. "He nearly knocked my head off that time! Thank goodness your dad is pulling this old chim down!"

"Dad can't do that!" cried Mayamiko. "Batty will fly away!"

"Good riddance!" said Mum. "What use is a creature like that? You tell me one good thing about him! He stinks like a monkey. Phew! And look at the mess he makes when he eats. He's worse than a parrot!"

Mayamiko wanted to say, "I'd like to see you try to eat a ripe mango – hanging upside down by your toes!"

He didn't dare say it. But the picture it put in his head made him giggle. He stuffed a fist into his mouth. But he couldn't seem to stop. . .

"You've got nothing to laugh about, boy!" said Mum, looking even more dangerous than usual. "You're in big trouble! Mrs Tambala wants a word with you!" She grabbed Mayamiko's arm.

But he twisted out of her grasp. He dodged past her. He ran past the mango tree, past Rinny shut up in her pen, and off into the bush.

Chapter 3

Leopard!

Darkness came in a sudden rush. Then the bush began to get really scary. But still Mayamiko didn't go home. He saw a big batty shape swooping across the moon.

"Is that you, Batty?" he called out to it.

But the shape flew on, into the night.

What's that? thought Mayamiko.

Something rustled in the long grass. Something howled in the distance – a long, spooky howl that made his skin crawl.

"I'd better go home now," Mayamiko decided.

He knew Mum and Dad and Anna would be frantic with worry. There

were leopards about. Last year, people said, one had even crept into a hut. It had snatched a new-born baby as it slept beside its mum. And the leopard was so sneaky, so quiet, that the mum didn't even wake up!

Mayamiko shivered. He stumbled along the track. There were green sparkles dancing in front of him.

Fireflies, thought Mayamiko. They cheered him up a bit.

Then something made his eyes dart sideways. Another pair of eyes stared back at him out of the dark. They glowed like two tiny golden lamps.

Leopard! thought Mayamiko.

He could hardly breathe. His chest felt tight as a puffed-up toad.

"Don't run!" Mayamiko warned himself. "Don't run! Be cool!"

If he ran, the leopard would come bursting out of the bush. It would chase him, spring on his back and kill him.

He forced himself to walk slowly. His legs were trembling like grass in the wind. He was amazed they were still holding him up.

He even managed to whistle a shaky little tune. As if to say, "Leopards? *Cha!* This boy is not afraid of leopards!"

The leopard was slinking after him. You couldn't see its body. Just eyes, floating in the dark. It could almost have been a ghost leopard. But Mayamiko knew it wasn't. It was a real leopard all right. Because it was doing what real leopards always do. It was sneaking closer and closer to Mayamiko. Moving in for the kill.

Mayamiko could see his house now. His legs were itching to run.

"Don't!" Mayamiko warned them.

"*Hack! Hack!*" A strange rasping noise came out of the bush. "*Hack! Hack!*" It was the leopard, coughing.

That did it. The animals went wild. There was a terrible racket. Baboons started barking. Other monkeys heard their alarm calls. They shrieked and hooted, "*Oo, oo, oo!*" like ghosts wailing in the dark.

Mayamiko panicked. He just couldn't help it.

He scooted towards his house. He wasn't going to make it. He could almost feel leopard-breath hot on his neck!

He dived through the curtain into the chim, rolled into a tight, shuddering ball and waited for those deadly claws to rake him.

Nothing happened.

Slowly, Mayamiko unrolled himself. Slowly, he stopped shaking.

"*Chink! Chink!*"

Mayamiko's heart jumped like a tree frog.

But it was only Batty, staring down at him with his big goggle eyes and friendly grin.

"Batty!" gabbled Mayamiko, relieved. "I thought you'd be out eating fruit. I'm being chased by a leopard, Batty. It followed me all the way home. But I think it's gone now."

Mayamiko spied out through the side of the curtain.

"It's okay, it's gone now," he told Batty.

He suddenly felt a lot better. He could even manage a little joke. "But I'd rather be chased by a leopard than by Mrs Tambala," he told Batty. "She's much more dangerous. She's more dangerous even than Mum! Eeee, she is one fierce woman!"

Then he stopped smiling. He said, "Oh, no!"

Two fiery eyes were staring out of the blackness under the mango tree. Mayamiko couldn't believe it. Quickly, he dropped the curtain.

"That leopard is still out there!"

What he didn't know was that the leopard was old and sick. And he was very, very hungry. He was desperate. Otherwise he wouldn't have risked coming so close to houses to look for food.

Mayamiko took another peek through the chim curtain.

But the leopard wasn't interested in him any more. He wasn't even looking in his direction. He'd found another meal. Rinny, the white goat, was lying in her pen. And the leopard's hungry eyes were gazing straight at her.

Chapter 4

Batty the Hero!

"What's wrong with Rinny?" Mayamiko asked Batty.

The old leopard had come into the open now. For the first time, Mayamiko could see his body. His spotty fur was mangy. His old bones ached. Some of his teeth were loose.

But when he glided towards that

pen, he still moved as smoothly as a river flows.

"Why is she lying down?" Mayamiko asked Batty. "Why isn't she making a big fuss? Why isn't she bleating so Mum can hear her?"

Then Mayamiko knew why. Rinny was having her babies. There was already one tiny kid by her side. It was new-born, still all floppy. Rinny was licking it clean.

"Mum! Dad!" yelled Mayamiko at the top of his voice.

But they didn't come out of the house.

"I've got to save Rinny and her baby," Mayamiko told Batty.

Batty was chinking like mad. As if he was warning Mayamiko not to do anything so crazy.

But then Mayamiko's mind was made up. For the door of his house opened. And only Anna came out. She peered around into the starry night, as if she was looking out for her brother.

Then she saw the leopard too. She saw him prowling round Rinny and her kid. Her mouth went into a big, round

"O". Her hand flew to her lips. She grabbed a twiggy broom.

"Oh, no," Mayamiko told Batty. "I can't believe it! She's going to try and chase the leopard away – with a broom!"

Batty rustled his bony wings as if he was as shocked as Mayamiko.

Anna shouted, "Hey!" at the leopard. She rushed forward. She shook the broom about.

The leopard looked at her in a lazy way. As if to say, "Who is this silly child? Trying to scare ME?"

Then he fixed his golden eyes on Rinny again. She was still lying on the ground. She was having another baby. Rinny always had twins.

One spring and the leopard would be inside the pen.

"Hey!" called Anna, shaking the broom and making another rush forward.

The leopard swung his head round. He stared at Anna again. As if he was thinking, "*Hummm*, which one shall I choose?"

Often, leopards didn't eat their prey straightaway. They dragged it off and hung it in a tree. Then chewed off a bit when they felt like it.

Mayamiko couldn't stay in the chim any longer. He had to do something – fast.

He yanked the curtain aside. Then charged out of the chim. He tried to scream like an angry elephant. Leopards are scared of elephants.

But his screams came out as mousy squeaks.

The old leopard swung his head. His blazing eyes burned into Mayamiko. Mayamiko stopped dead. He couldn't move. He just stood there, shaking. He thought, I'm in big trouble now!

Even Anna seemed frozen, her broom

held high above her head. Her eyes were wide with horror. She watched the leopard take a few lazy steps towards Mayamiko. Then she saw his muscles bunch up under his skin. He was going to attack!

Anna shrieked. But it didn't make any difference. The leopard didn't care about her any more. He was only interested in Mayamiko. He'd decided he was easy prey.

Now he'd make up his mind he didn't mess around. The leopard exploded into action. He was old. But still quick as lightning in a short sprint. Just a blur of golden fur and dust. Faster than your eye could follow.

And Mayamiko just stood there, helpless!

Whoosh! Something shot out of the chim. It was cackling like mad. It had glittering, goggly eyes. It clattered on great leathery wings.

The leopard skidded to a stop. His claws made long rakes in the dust.

The cackling, flapping thing dived low. It almost parted his hair!

In one smooth movement the leopard spun round. His body did a loop-the-loop! He was off. He'd had enough. He snarled: "*Rrrrrrr*." Then slid back into the bush, as silently as a ghost.

Chapter 5

Batty is Saved!

Batty was chinking in the mango tree. Rinny was licking her twin kids. Anna had put the twiggy broom back. The excitement was all over when Mum and Dad came rushing round the corner of the house.

"Where have you been?" yelled Mum as soon as she set eyes on

Mayamiko. "We've been out looking for you everywhere!" She looked as if she didn't know whether to slap him, or hug him. "We were worried sick!"

"Mr Gomesi says he saw a leopard hanging around the place," added Dad.

"I know," said Mayamiko. "It was here a minute ago. Right under that mango tree."

"You're kidding us!" said Mum.

"No, no," said Anna. "Truly! It was going to eat Rinny and her new babies. And we tried to stop it. So then it decided to eat Mayamiko instead!"

"And Batty stopped it," said Mayamiko proudly. "He came diving out of the chim. You should have seen him. He scared that leopard away. He was a hero!"

Mum gave Dad a glance as if to say: "What will that boy dream up next?"

"It's true!" said Anna. "I saw it!"

"So please, Dad," begged Mayamiko. "Don't pull the old chim down. Let Batty stay. Please Dad, please!"

Dad looked at Mum. He raised his eyebrows. He gave a big shrug.

"Please," said Mayamiko, turning to Mum. "You wanted to know one good thing about Batty. Well, he scares leopards away. That's a really good thing, isn't it?"

"And he saved Mayamiko's life," added Anna.

Mum tutted. She frowned. She shook her head. She screwed her mouth up as if she was sucking a lime.

Mayamiko thought, She's going to say no!

But when Mum opened her mouth she said, "I suppose we must give this Batty a home then, if he saved my son's life."

Mayamiko went wild with delight. He did several great, springy leaps. He hugged himself. He punched the air.

"Yay!" When he calmed down he said, "Thanks, Mum."

When Mum had gone, Mayamiko called up into the mango tree.

"Batty! Batty!" he called softly. "Did you hear what Mum said? She said the old chim can stay. And you can stay too!"

From high up in the tree came a rustle of wings.

"*Chink! Chink!*"

Then a bit of ripe mango came plopping down through the branches. And landed squelch! at Mayamiko's feet.

A few days later, Mayamiko was round at Bernard's house.

He had to go to the chim in Bernard's back yard. When he came out, Bernard was laughing at him. He was laughing so hard he was clutching his belly and rolling round in the dust.

"You – you – you!" he gasped, pointing helplessly at his cousin.

"What? What?" said a bewildered Mayamiko. "What's so funny?"

When Bernard could talk, he said, "Don't you know what you did? Before you went into our chim?"

"No," said Mayamiko, still puzzled.

Bernard got up off the ground. "Just watch me," he said. "I'll show you."

Bernard walked, quite normally, up to the chim. Then, suddenly, he kicked the door open, dropped into a crouch and wrapped his arms round his head like a turban.

"You did that!" said Bernard, starting to giggle all over again. "Why did you do that? You looked really ridiculous!"

"Oh, that!" said Mayamiko. "I always do that when I go into chims. Just in case."

"What do you mean, my crazy cousin?" asked Bernard. "What do you mean, just in case?"

"Just in case a giant fruit bat flies out and knocks my head off."

"Oh," said Bernard. He was still grinning. But his grin looked a little bit shaky.

After Mayamiko went home, Bernard paid a visit to the chim.

As he was walking across the yard, he remembered his big cousin's warning. Bernard thought, What a load of old rubbish! There's never been a giant fruit bat in our chim!

He put his hand on the door. He hesitated. He just couldn't help worrying. He was thinking, On the other hand, you can't be too careful. I don't want to get my head knocked off. . .

Mrs Tambala was sitting on her front step. She'd done all her chores. She was sipping a glass of beer.

She watched Bernard walking to his chim. Then her eyes boggled. Her mouth dropped open in amazement. "What is that boy doing?" she asked herself, as Bernard kicked the chim door open, then dived to the ground with his head in his hands. She shook her head sadly. "Children these days!" she said. "They are all totally round the bend!"

Author's Note.

Dear Reader, please don't be alarmed by this story. You can visit your own chim quite safely. No giant fruit bat with goggly eyes and great, black wings will come swooping out and knock your head off. You can be sure of that. Especially if you *never* forget to kick the door open and duck. . .

The End